MICHAEL DAHL PRESENTS

MYSTERIES

BY BRANDON TERRELL

ILLUSTRATED BY AMERIGO PINELLI

STONE ARCH BOOKS
a capstone imprint

Michael Dahl Presents is published by Stone Arch Books,
an imprint of Capstone.
1710 Roe Crest Drive
North Mankato, Minnesota 56003
www.capstonepub.com

Library of Congress Cataloging-in-Publication Data is available on the Library of Congress website.

ISBN: 978-1-4965-9705-2 (library binding)
ISBN: 978-1-4965-9886-8 (paperback)
ISBN: 978-1-4965-9730-4 (eBook PDF)

Summary: Ellis Baker is excited to go on her family vacation. But during the dark and stormy overnight flight, one passenger's priceless necklace mysteriously disappears. Even spookier is the bizarre woman who also disappears without a trace. Could the stranger have stolen the necklace and somehow gotten off the plane? Or was the strange woman really a ghost with a taste for fancy jewelry?

Editor: Aaron Sautter
Designer: Lori Bye
Production Specialist: Tori Abraham

Printed in the United States of America.
PA117

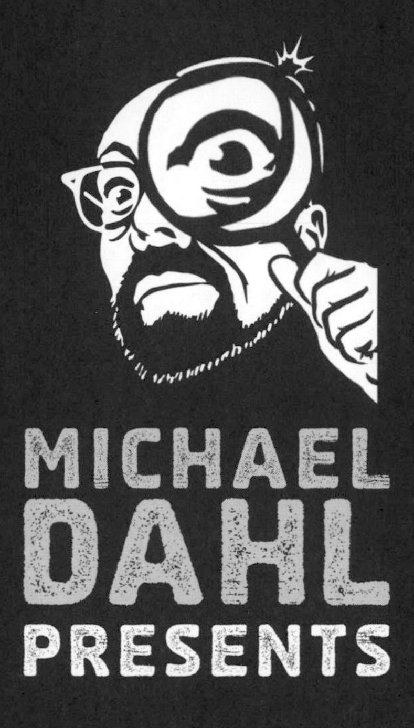

Michael Dahl has written about werewolves, magicians, and superheroes. He loves funny books, scary books, and mysterious books. Every Michael Dahl Presents book is chosen by Michael himself and written by an author he loves. The books are about favorite subjects like monster aliens, haunted houses, farting pigs, or magical powers that go haywire. Read on!

DETECTIVES OF THE IMPOSSIBLE

Sherlock Holmes is my hero. He is the Great Detective. I discovered him back in the 4th grade, and I've been reading about his adventures ever since. He can solve the most puzzling mysteries from the tiniest of clues. Nothing is impossible to him.

BUT—could Sherlock solve the weird, modern mysteries in these books? Could he figure out how a passenger disappears from a plane that's flying 30,000 feet in the air? Could he solve the puzzle of how a person seems to shrink to microscopic size? Would he crack the cases of a dead body that falls out of an empty cabinet, or how someone is poisoned inside a locked room? Read on and see if you can outdo Sherlock by solving these mysteries yourself. Or . . . are they simply impossible?

TABLE OF CONTENTS

Chapter One

BOARDING CALL

"May I have your attention please?" the ticketing agent said into the microphone. "Flight 1015 with non-stop overnight service from New York to Los Angeles will begin boarding in ten minutes."

Thirteen-year old Ellis Baker looked up from the book she was reading. It was a Kerri Keane mystery, her all-time favorite book series. "About time," she whispered.

Ellis and her parents had been waiting at the airport gate for nearly an hour. Her dad always stressed the importance of arriving early.

"If you're on time," he'd say, "you're late." He said it every time he had to go somewhere important.

This was one of those times. Ellis and her parents were flying cross-country so her dad could give a speech for some convention named Chet Chats. "My lecture will be broadcasted live on the Web," he'd explained. "Who knows how many people will see it?!"

Ellis's dad was seated in one of the red chairs across from her. His eyes were glued to his laptop. She watched his pupils travel left to right, saw his lips moving ever so slightly as he read his speech for the umpteenth time.

Ellis's mom sat next to him, leafing through a thick design magazine. It was almost midnight . . . *way* past Ellis's bedtime. At this time of night, the terminal was like a ghost town. Just a few people were seated at high tables near a row of vending machines. A few more sat in the chairs around them.

As they waited, a soft plinking sound began to fill the terminal. Ellis looked at the large windows facing the tarmac. Raindrops were streaking down the windows in thin rows.

"Well that's just great," said an older woman seated next to a window. Ellis wasn't sure who she was speaking to; the woman sat alone.

Maybe she's talking to her dog? Ellis thought.

The woman had a small dog carrier in her lap. She looked nervously out the window, her fingers lightly touching her necklace. And what a necklace! Ellis had never seen one like it before. It sparkled with a stunning, heart-shaped blue jewel hanging from a chain of pearls. It was definitely *not* the kind of necklace you wear to an airport at midnight.

Ellis was ready to be in the air. She looked forward to more than six hours of reading, watching movies, and *sleeping*. She raised her book and was about to start reading when—

"Hey! Watch it!"

Ellis looked up to see a man in a rumpled suit at one of the high tables nearby. He was speaking to a boy who was about Ellis's age. The boy wore a cap and a loose jacket, and his eyes were wide with fright.

"I'm sorry, sir," the boy said. The man was using napkins to sop up spilled coffee on the table. "I didn't mean to run into you."

"It's fine, *fine*," the man grumbled. His mustache waggled comically.

Ellis was about to return to her book when she noticed something odd about the scene. While the man was distracted by his spilled drink, the boy reached into the man's suit coat

MY PET

pocket and neatly plucked out his wallet. Then, as smooth as silk, the boy simply strolled away.

Ellis's jaw dropped. The man had been robbed! She needed to say something to the man, or at least to the woman taking tickets. But Ellis could no longer see the thief. She opened her mouth to tell her parents about him. But then the ticketing agent spoke again into the microphone.

"We will now begin boarding Flight 1015," she said. "Thank you so much for your patience."

BOOM!

As the agent finished her announcement, a clap of thunder rumbled through the terminal.

Chapter Two

THE PALE WOMAN

Ellis shoved her Kerri Keane novel into the rainbow backpack at her feet. When she stood up, she looked for the thief in the cap, but he was nowhere to be seen. She and her parents then joined the small line of passengers waiting to get on the plane. Ellis stood behind the woman with the beautiful blue-jeweled necklace.

The woman cradled her dog carrier in her arms like it was a baby. When she reached the front of the line, she gently set down the dog carrier. Then she fumbled around in her purse before pulling out her plane ticket.

"Bernice Waterson?" the ticketing agent asked the woman.

"Yes," she replied.

"Welcome aboard." The ticketing agent scanned her ticket and handed it back.

Ellis and her parents followed with the other passengers. They handed their tickets to the agent, then walked down the narrow hallway to their plane.

For a cross-country flight, the plane was quite large. It seemed strange to Ellis that so few passengers were boarding such a big plane.

Why aren't there more people here? she wondered. *Maybe because it's a red-eye flight.*

The lights in the plane were dimmed, creating a soothing atmosphere for people who wanted to sleep. Ellis walked carefully down the narrow aisle until she reached her row. As she waited for her parents to cram into their seats, Ellis glanced over at the boarding passengers. Her breath caught in her throat.

There he is! she gasped to herself.

The thief from earlier casually strolled onto the plane. It looked like he was traveling alone. Like Ellis, he carried a backpack. But his was covered in patches and small buttons.

She watched as he walked past the row where Bernice Waterson sat. Ellis noticed that the boy stopped and stared way too long at the woman. He was clearly sizing up her impressive jewelry.

As he continued down the aisle, Ellis realized *he was walking right toward her.* She quickly plopped down into her seat to avoid him and fumbled with her seatbelt as he passed.

"Need help?" her dad joked. He was already setting up his laptop on the seat-back tray.

"I'm fine," Ellis said.

She tried hard not to turn around to see where the boy was sitting.

After a few minutes the flight crew began closing the overhead storage bins to prepare for takeoff. One of them asked Ellis's dad to put his seat-tray back in place. Ellis shut her eyes and took a deep breath of stale airplane air. When she opened them again, she looked around and noticed one last passenger settling into her seat.

It was hard *not* to notice the woman. She had very dark hair with bangs that covered her forehead, and her skin was incredibly pale. She wore a thick leopard-print coat and cat's-eye-shaped sunglasses.

That's strange. Who wears sunglasses at night? Ellis wondered.

Ellis couldn't take her eyes off the pale woman. She moved in smooth, careful steps.

No one but Ellis seemed to see her. The woman slipped into the seat next to Bernice Waterson, who didn't even move, much less greet the woman.

That's so strange, Ellis thought. *Or maybe I'm just tired. Everything about this crazy late-night flight is weirding me out.*

The pilot's voice then came over the loudspeaker. "Please prepare for takeoff."

Ellis decided to dig her Kerri Keane mystery out of her backpack. Then she aimed the small light above her to shine down properly and started to read. It was going to be a long flight.

Chapter Three

TURBULENCE

BRRRMMMMBBBLL! THUMP!

Ellis jerked awake as a clap of thunder shook the plane. Her Kerri Keane mystery had slipped from her lap and fallen loudly to the floor.

"Wha . . . ?" Ellis rubbed her eyes and shifted in her seat. Her still-sleepy brain tried to figure out what was happening. She checked her watch. They'd been in the air for only an hour. There were still five hours left.

A passing crew member stooped over and picked up the book. She handed it to Ellis and tucked a stray strand of blond hair behind one ear. Ellis noticed a smudge of something white along her jawline. "It's okay. It's just a little turbulence," the woman explained.

A little? Ellis thought as the plane shuddered again. She gripped her seat's armrests and looked toward her parents. They were both asleep and weren't fazed by the plane's shaking.

An orange light went on above her, followed by a soft ping. "Attention please," the pilot's voice said calmly. "We're hitting a stretch of rough weather. Please stay in your seats while the 'Fasten Seatbelt' light is on. Thank you."

Ellis peered past her sleeping parents and out the plane window. As she did, a crack of lightning flickered across the clouds.

The airplane shook again.

Ellis glanced around the plane. Many of the passengers were sleeping through the turbulence. She noticed that the thief was awake. He wore a set of headphones and was staring at the small screen in front of him. The light from the screen danced off his face. Suddenly he looked up and glanced at Ellis. It was like he could sense that she was spying on him. She quickly looked away.

Bernice Waterson appeared to be sleeping as well. Her dog didn't seem worried by the rough weather, though. It hadn't made a peep since they got on the plane. In fact, Ellis couldn't remember the dog barking *at all* since she'd first seen Ms. Waterson.

The seat next to Ms. Waterson was now empty. The odd pale woman was gone.

Where did she go? Ellis thought. *The pilot said to remain in our seats.*

KA-BOOM!

Another flash of lightning lit up the sky outside. A crack of thunder echoed around the airplane. A bout of shaking followed, causing the plane to dip violently. Ellis's stomach fluttered like when she rode the big roller coaster at the amusement park.

"Hmm . . ." Ellis's dad muttered. The jolt was enough to wake several of the sleeping passengers, including her dad. He wiped a bit of drool from the corner of his mouth. The air in the plane felt electric as more passengers whispered about the storm and shifted in their seats.

And then from out of nowhere came a blood-curdling scream. It was Bernice Waterson. "AAAAGGHH!" she shouted. "My necklace—it's gone!"

Chapter Four

DISAPPEARANCES

Ms. Waterson's scream woke many of the other passengers. Ellis's mom peeled off her eye mask. "Heavens, what's wrong?" she asked groggily.

Ellis sat up straighter. "The woman with the dog," she said. "She was wearing an amazing blue necklace. It's missing!"

It sounded like something from one of Ellis's favorite Kerri Keane mysteries. Nearly the same thing had happened in *The Clue in the Lost Locket*. Except that the stolen jewelry had been a girl's locket. And the story took place in a haunted castle instead of an airplane. Still, Ellis was excited by the mystery.

"I'm sure it'll be found," Ellis's mom said. She slid the eye mask down and leaned back again. "We're on an airplane. It's not like it can just vanish."

Her mom was probably right, but Ellis remained curious. Flight crew members were huddled around Bernice Waterson. She was wildly flinging her hands around while telling them about her missing necklace. They spoke in hushed tones, but Ellis could faintly hear them.

"Please ma'am," a female crew member with a black ponytail said. "Just calm down."

"But that necklace . . . it's been in my family for generations!" Ms. Waterson said.

"Have you checked the area around your seat?" a bald male crew member asked. He squatted down and began searching the floor.

"It's not there!" Ms. Waterson was becoming more frantic.

"It's okay, ma'am," a man said as he approached the group. He had a mustache and wore a rumpled suit. "I'm the air marshal. Maybe I can be of some help."

Ellis's jaw dropped open. It was the man from the airport whose wallet was stolen! She glanced toward the thief. He was also intently watching the air marshal. One of the boy's feet shoved his backpack as far under his seat as possible. He looked over, and he and Ellis locked eyes. Ellis quickly turned away.

"The woman sitting next to me," Bernice Waterson continued. "*She* must have it."

"Woman next to you?" The air marshal looked puzzled. "There's no one there."

"But she was here earlier," Ms. Waterson protested.

"And did you speak to this woman?" the bald man asked.

Ms. Waterson thought a moment, then shook her head.

"I don't recall seeing anyone in that seat," the bald man said.

"She was here before, I swear," Ms. Waterson replied. "But she's gone now. Why would she take my necklace? And how does someone just disappear at 30,000 feet?"

"*I* know," a voice beside Ellis whispered, startling her. She turned and was shocked to see the thief sitting across the aisle from her.

Ellis was too surprised to speak. After a moment, she croaked, "What?"

"I know how that woman disappeared," the thief said with a smile. He wiggled his fingers dramatically. "Because she was never there. She's a *ghost*!"

Chapter Five

THE THIEF AND THE GHOST

Ellis gasped.

A ghost?! No way! It was just like the Kerri Keane novel *Haunting at Hillbrook Manor*. Except, of course, this ghost was a strangely dressed woman and not a dead butler.

The thief stared at Ellis as she worked things out in her head. Then he burst out laughing. "Man, I really had you there," he said. "You don't believe in ghosts, do you?"

Ellis shrugged. "Maybe?"

"And what? They're just hanging out with their best pals Bigfoot and the Loch Ness Monster?" he said, chuckling with a big grin.

Ellis rolled her eyes and tried to ignore the boy. She turned her attention back to the crew members questioning Ms. Waterson.

"I'm Luke, by the way," the thief said.

Ellis didn't respond.

Luke leaned in closer, peering at her book. "Kerri Keane, eh? Never read 'em. Mysteries, right?"

"I know what you did," Ellis said abruptly. She slid her book off her lap, away from where Luke could see it.

"What I did?"

"The air marshal," Ellis said sternly. "I saw you take his wallet."

"I don't know what you're talking about."

"Very funny. I should go over and tell him right now."

"Because you think that's what he'd be worried about?" Luke replied. He didn't look too concerned. "Go for it, Kerri Keane."

"My name is Ellis." It slipped out before she could stop herself.

Luke smiled. "Nice to meet you, Ellis. So, do you really think that woman just disappeared?"

"Where could she be?" Ellis answered. "There aren't many places someone can hide on an airplane."

"I'm pretty sure I saw her walking down the aisle earlier," Luke said.

"You did?"

He nodded. "I think she was heading to the bathroom. Maybe. I mean, old people, you know. Always using the bathroom."

"Gross."

"I wasn't paying attention, though," Luke continued. "I was watching the new *Ninja Mummy* movie."

Another burst of lightning crackled outside, making the plane dip and rattle. The crew members next to Bernice Waterson grabbed the back of the nearest seats to steady themselves. The air marshal stumbled but caught himself.

"Whoa," Luke said. "That was a big one. Between the rough weather and the ghosts, I guess I should have taken an earlier flight."

Ellis thought back to when they boarded the plane. The pale woman had been the last to arrive. And Bernice Waterson had never even noticed her. And now she seemed to have vanished into thin air.

Maybe she was *a ghost?* Ellis thought. *But if she was, then why was the necklace missing?*

There had to be a logical reason for everything. Ellis decided that she was going to get to the bottom of this mystery. And to do so, she'd have to talk to Bernice Waterson.

Chapter Six

CHANNELING KERRI KEANE

In every Kerri Keane mystery, the junior detective interviewed the victim to get more information. In one story she spoke with a mansion owner about a stolen rare diamond. In another she talked to a farmer in a muddy barnyard about his missing prized pig. In one spooky mystery she questioned a movie director on a film set that was supposedly cursed.

Ellis wanted very much to be like Kerri and speak to Bernice Waterson. But she needed to be patient.

Besides, unlike Luke, who did whatever he wanted, Ellis wasn't a rule breaker. She was going to stay in her seat while the "Fasten Seatbelt" light was on.

So she waited. She read her book for a bit and then pretended to fall asleep. She hoped Luke would get bored and return to his own seat. Eventually, he did. A short while later, after the plane had been cruising smoothly for several minutes, the seatbelt light went off.

Ellis cracked open her eyes. Sure enough, Bernice Waterson was still awake.

Here goes nothing, she thought.

Ellis untied one of her sneakers, then got up and slowly walked down the aisle. When she reached Bernice Waterson's row, she pretended to notice the untied shoe.

"Oh no," she said. "How did *that* happen?" Ellis sat in the empty seat across the aisle from Bernice Waterson as she retied her purple shoelaces.

When she was finished, she looked up and said, "Hi. So . . . um . . . did they find your necklace?"

Ms. Waterson seemed taken aback for a second. Then she said, "No. They have not."

"I heard you say something about a woman sitting next to you. Do you think *she* took it?"

Ms. Waterson eyed Ellis warily for a second. She must have decided that the girl wasn't pestering her too much, because she nodded. "I'm certain of it."

"But where could she have gone?"

Ms. Waterson shrugged. "I never should have worn the necklace at all," she said. "It's been in my family for generations. I thought wearing it would be safer than shipping it. Such a foolish move. Thank goodness it's insured."

Ms. Waterson dropped her head into her hands and began to cry softly. Ellis felt uncomfortable. Being Kerri Keane was harder than she thought.

"I'm sure they'll find it," she said timidly.

Just then the plane was rocked by another crack of thunder. It was the first in a long while. It had been so long that Ellis was surprised by the new rough patch.

Ms. Waterson gripped the dog carrier in her lap. Ellis nodded at it. "At least your dog is keeping calm in this bad weather," she said. "My cousin's dog hates thunderstorms. Oh, and fireworks on the Fourth of July. Basically, he runs and hides under the bed from any loud noise."

Ms. Waterson sniffled. "Yes, well, Princess is always okie-dokie," she replied.

The "Fasten Seatbelt" light pinged on. At the same time, the dark-haired crew member stopped

beside them. She held a slip of paper as she looked at Ellis. "Please return to your seat," she said.

"Yes, ma'am," Ellis said, standing. But she paused a moment before returning to her seat.

The woman then turned to Ms. Waterson. "I've checked this flight list," she explained. "There's no record of anyone assigned to the seat next to you. The woman you spoke of . . . she doesn't exist."

Ellis cast a glance toward Luke. He was awake and was also listening to the two women talking. When he noticed Ellis looking at him, his lips formed one single word.

Ghost.

Chapter Seven

LUKE THE LIAR?

Ellis slumped back into her seat and clicked her seatbelt. She'd hoped that talking with Bernice Waterson would have revealed some clues. But she ended up talking about her cousin's dog Rosco as much as the missing necklace. She hadn't learned much at all.

That's a mistake Kerri Keane would never make, Ellis thought.

In a while the rough weather settled down. The crew members soon wheeled their drink carts down the aisles. Ellis decided she needed an energy boost. She definitely didn't want to sleep through the rest of the flight.

Two crew members, the bald man and the ponytailed woman, pushed a cart toward her. It wobbled and squeaked.

"Can I get you anything?" the man asked her.

"A soda, please," Ellis replied.

As the man cracked open a can and filled a cup, he spoke to his coworker. "This whole trip has been strange," he muttered. "First Vanessa doesn't show up, and we have to fly in bad weather. Then that whole necklace thing happened. I feel like this whole flight is cursed or something."

"It's just nerves," the ponytailed woman replied. "Besides, Vanessa is here."

"She is?"

"Yep. You probably didn't recognize her with blond hair."

"Huh." The bald man finished pouring the soda into the cup and passed the fizzing beverage to Ellis.

"Thank you," Ellis said.

The man smiled and then pushed the cart forward.

This was by far the strangest flight Ellis had ever been on. And it was clear that she wasn't the only one who felt that way. The crew seemed on edge, sensing the eerie vibes throughout the plane.

Ellis sipped her soda. The rush of sugar from her bubbly drink was just what she needed. But when she cracked open her Kerri Keane novel, she just couldn't seem to focus on the words.

Maybe I should watch a movie instead, she thought.

Ellis dug her headphones out of her backpack and plugged them into the jack on the armrest.

She settled them over her ears and turned on the screen in front of her. Most of the movies didn't look very interesting to her. Action. Talking cat. Remake of some movie from years ago.

What about the new Ninja Mummy *movie?* she thought. She remembered the film Luke had mentioned watching earlier.

Ellis went to the search screen and typed in the movie's title. NO RESULTS FOUND, the screen said.

"That's odd," Ellis muttered.

Ellis looked back at Luke. He was sleeping with his mouth open and his cap pulled down over his eyes.

He was lying to me, Ellis concluded. *But why?*

earch NO RESULTS FOUND

Chapter Eight

AN EMBARRASSING DISCOVERY

Luke had lied to Ellis since the first time they spoke. He claimed not to know about the air marshal's wallet. He said he was watching a *Ninja Mummy* movie when he clearly wasn't.

What else was he lying about?

Maybe he has the necklace right alongside the wallet in his backpack, Ellis thought. *He is a thief, after all.*

Ellis took one last swig of her soda, then went over to Luke's row. She sat heavily in the seat next to him.

"Huh? Wha-zzit?" Luke snorted and sat up. He looked around, not realizing that his cap was pulled over his eyes.

Finally, he pushed the cap up and saw Ellis staring at him. "Oh," he said. "It's you. What's up, Kerri Keane?"

"It was you. You stole the necklace, didn't you?" Ellis asked.

"Whoa," Luke replied. "That was subtle."

"Admit it. You have the necklace stashed away with the wallet." She reached down and pulled his backpack from under his seat. "They're both right here, right?"

"Hey!" Luke snatched the backpack from her. A button with a smiley face that read *Joke's on You!* laughed back at Ellis.

"Hands off," he said. "My backpack is none of your beeswax."

"I should just call the air marshal over," Ellis said. "He can check for the necklace himself."

She began to stand, raising her hand to wave at the air marshal. Luke grabbed her arm and pulled her back down. "Stop," he said. "Just . . . you know what? Fine. You wanna see my backpack, here you go."

Luke unzipped his backpack. It was messy inside. A sweatshirt was crammed at the bottom. There was also a small, clear bag with a toothbrush and floss inside. A paperback copy of *On the Road* sat to one side. There was definitely no necklace.

Ellis's cheeks burned red. "I'm . . ."

"Not Kerri Keane," he finished. But he was smiling, which meant he wasn't too upset.

"But *Ninja Mummy,*" Ellis stammered. "You said you were watching it."

"Well *yeah,*" Luke said. "You think I'd tell you what I was *really* watching?" He tapped the screen in front of him. An image labeled RECENTLY VIEWED popped up.

It showed the poster for a romance movie titled *Duchess in Love*. It featured a man in a suit and a woman in a big puffy dress. They were kissing under some beautiful flowers.

"Now you know my embarrassing secret," Luke said. "I like cheesy love stories."

Ellis slapped her hand over her mouth before she could laugh. It was too funny, though, and she couldn't help herself. She snickered and felt a full-fledged laugh about to break free.

Just then the plane dipped fiercely, followed by the worst rattling they'd felt in the past four hours. A woman screamed. The oxygen masks above them dropped down all at once. Then the doors for the overhead storage sprang open. People's belongings spilled out onto the seats and into the aisles!

Chapter Nine

THE FINAL CLUES

"Everyone please remain calm!" the bald crew member shouted. His beverage cart rolled down the aisle and hit the back of an empty seat. The other crew members scrambled to close overhead bins and scoop up stray bags and coats.

"Ellis?!"

Ellis's mom sprang out of her seat, the neck pillow still snug around her neck. She twisted one way, then the other, searching for her daughter. If the situation was different, Ellis would find it funny.

"I'm here, Mom!" Ellis waved at her mom as the plane leveled out. She stood and began to work her way back toward her seat. Two small suitcases, one blue, one dark green, lay in her path. Also, a garbage bag filled with clothes was in the aisle. She couldn't get to her seat until they'd been picked up.

"Please relax," the bald man said. "There's no need to use the oxygen masks. We'll be okay."

Another flash of lightning shot through the sky outside.

The blond woman hurried over. Ellis could clearly read her name badge now. It read "Vanessa." Vanessa stopped at the garbage bag of clothes and quickly glanced left and right. Then she scooped the bag up in her arms.

"Don't you folks worry," Vanessa said, looking around at the passengers. Then she flashed a nervous smile. "Everything's okie-dokie."

CRACK!

More lightning and thunder. In the bright flash of light, Ellis caught a glimpse of some animal-print clothing in the garbage bag. Vanessa quickly retied the bag and shoved it back into an overhead bin. Ellis, puzzled by the sight, sat back down beside Luke.

"Sorry about that, folks," the pilot's soothing voice came over the speakers. "I've got good news, though. We're approaching the end of our flight, and it's clear skies ahead."

Luke sighed. "Finally," he said. "I'm going to use the bathroom. I mean, on a flight this long, *everyone* has to go eventually. Am I right?"

"Ugh," Ellis said. "TMI."

She stood to let Luke out into the aisle. As she did, Ellis glanced up at Bernice Waterson. The woman was still cradling Princess's dog carrier. Luke's words echoed in her head, and

Ellis thought about everything she'd seen and heard during the flight.

Then, as it often happened near the end of every Kerri Keane novel, a lightbulb switched on in Ellis's head. The whole mystery of the missing necklace clicked into place.

She'd figured the whole thing out!

DID YOU SOLVE THE MYSTERY?

What We Know:

- Before boarding the plane, Ellis saw Luke steal the air marshal's wallet.
- As they boarded the plane, a mysterious woman with pale skin and a leopard-print coat sat next to Bernice Waterson.
- Ms. Waterson's dog is very quiet throughout the flight, in spite of the stormy weather.
- Sometime during the flight, Ms. Waterson's valuable blue-jeweled necklace was stolen. At the same time, the pale-skinned woman seems to have vanished from the plane.

- After talking with Luke, Ellis realized that he lied about several things. She suspects that he might have stolen the necklace.

Were you able to figure out the clues and solve the mystery? Who stole Ms. Waterson's expensive necklace? Who was the pale woman, and how did she disappear from the plane at 30,000 feet? Was she really a ghost? And if so, why would she want to steal a fancy necklace?

Chapter Ten

BUSTED!

The plane landed in Los Angeles less than an hour later. Its wheels squealed as they touched down on the tarmac. The storm had passed, and the pale dawn light was beginning to brighten the sky.

"Good morning folks. Welcome to Los Angeles," the pilot said.

Groggy travelers stood and gathered their things. Ellis saw Luke shoulder his backpack and hurry off the plane.

He's scared, Ellis thought. Earlier she'd told him what she thought happened to the necklace. And she had said she would tell the air marshal. Luke had seemed skittish and nervous.

"Ready, hon?" Ellis's dad asked. His eyes were bloodshot. *Huh,* she thought. *I guess that's why they call these overnight flights "red-eyes."*

After Ellis and her parents left the plane, she saw the air marshal talking to Bernice Waterson. He was asking a few last questions and writing info down in a small notebook.

Ellis tried to work up the courage to speak with them. But as she did, she was stunned to see Luke walking over to the air marshal.

"Excuse me?" Luke said.

"Yes?" the air marshal replied, his mustache curling ever so slightly. Clearly, he recognized the boy who'd knocked over his pre-flight beverage.

Luke held out the man's wallet. "I . . . uh, I noticed you dropped this on your way off the plane."

The air marshal's eyes widened. "Oh," he said, taking the wallet from Luke. "Oh wow. Thank you, young man."

"It was nothing." Luke nodded in Ellis's direction. "By the way, I think my friend over there might know what happened to the necklace."

Bernice Waterson and the air marshal turned to look at her.

"Gimme a second," Ellis told her tired parents. Then she joined the other group.

"You . . . know what happened to my necklace?" Bernice Waterson asked, clutching her dog carrier.

"Yes," Ellis said.

"Please explain," said the air marshal.

"Well, you know that woman Vanessa? The blond crew member?"

The air marshal nodded.

"*She's* the missing woman."

Bernice Waterson gasped.

"How do you know this?" the air marshal asked, raising an eyebrow.

"I overheard two of the crew who were confused about whether or not she was onboard," Ellis said.

"And when she helped me with my book," Ellis continued, "I saw a smudge of white makeup on her cheek." She knew she had cracked the case, just like Kerri Keane. "She must have missed a spot wiping it off. The makeup was part of her disguise to make her look pale. And as a crew member, she knew which seats would be empty. So she took the one next to Ms. Waterson."

The air marshal looked impressed.

"Plus," Ellis continued. "When that bag of clothes fell out of an overhead bin, I saw her leopard-print coat."

"Well," Ms. Waterson said. "If she *was* the thief, then where did she hide the necklace?"

"Oh, you already know the answer," Ellis said with a smile. "Because it was never stolen."

Luke chuckled. "Gotcha," he said.

Ellis pointed at the dog carrier. "Princess did so good during the whole flight. She didn't fuss or bark or need to go to the bathroom at all. And it was a *long* flight. *Everybody* needs to use the bathroom eventually. Even dogs."

Ellis peered through the door of the dog carrier in Ms. Waterson's arms. Sure enough, there wasn't a dog in it at all! There *was*, however, a glittering blue necklace resting on a small dog bed.

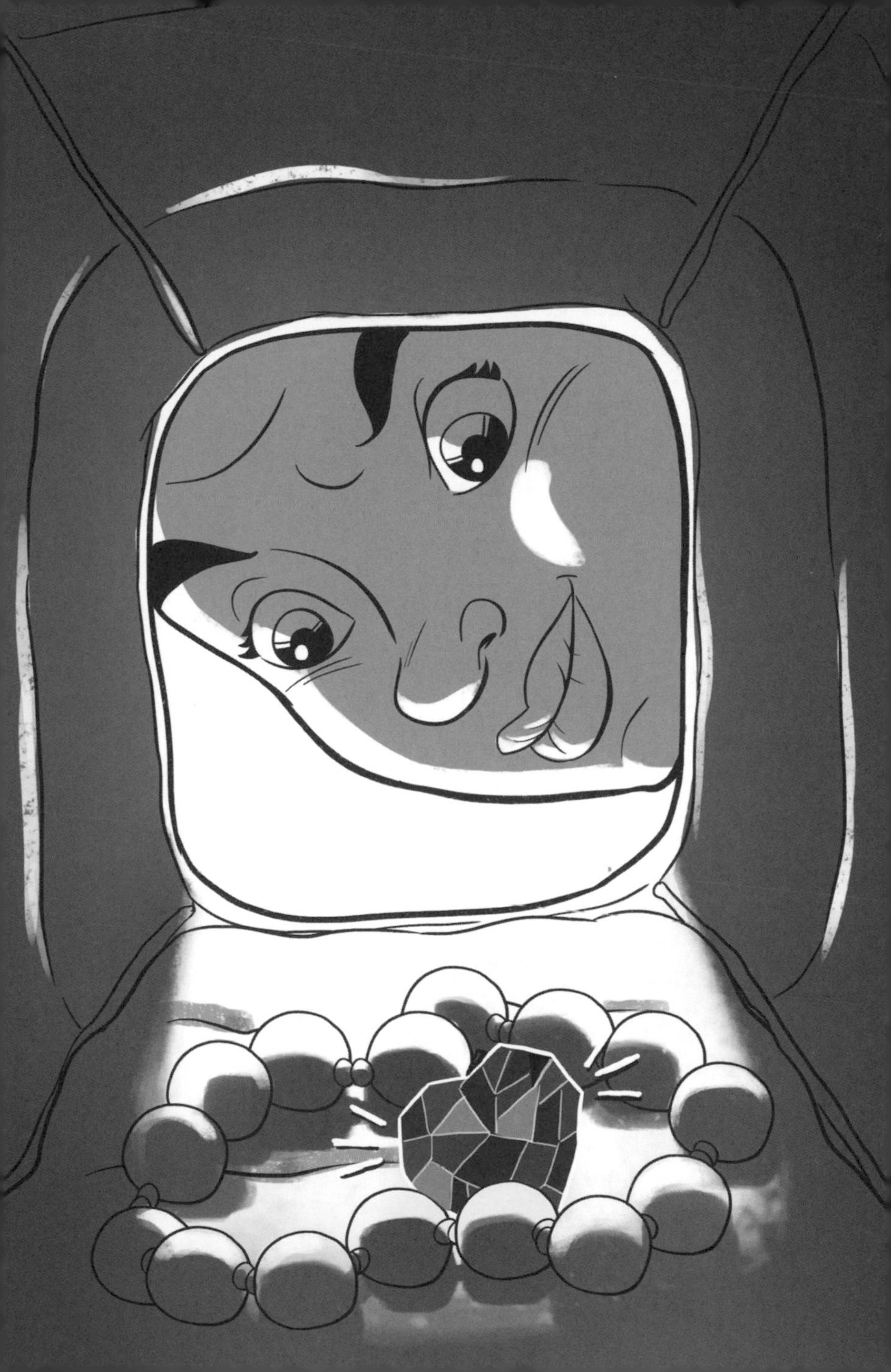

"Bingo," Ellis said.

The air marshal flipped his notebook closed. "Ma'am," he said to Ms. Waterson, "I think we need to have a very different conversation."

"And you may wanna talk to *her*, too," Luke added, pointing at the gate. Vanessa was wheeling a small suitcase quickly into the terminal.

"She's your sister, right?" Ellis said. "You both talk alike. Anyway, your scheme almost worked. You pretended that the necklace was stolen by a mysterious stranger who just disappeared. But you really just stashed it in your dog carrier.

"I'm guessing you were going to cash in the insurance claim on the necklace. You'd get the money and keep the necklace for yourself. Everything would be 'okie-dokie' then." She smiled at her own joke.

Bernice Waterson glared at her, lip curled in a sneer. "You clever kids," she muttered.

The air marshal raised a hand to flag down Vanessa. "Excuse me," he said. "Can I speak with you for a moment?"

Ellis and Luke slowly backed away as the air marshal grilled the two women. As they did, Ellis turned and asked, "So are you bummed?"

"About what?" Luke asked. "Giving back the wallet?"

"No. That the pale woman wasn't a ghost after all."

"Nah," Luke said. "Turns out seeing a teen detective solve a mid-flight mystery is cooler than any haunted airplane."

Luke smiled and adjusted his backpack. "Nice work, Kerri Keane."

Ellis smiled back. "Thanks."

Luke walked away, blending in with the other tired travelers. Ellis watched until he disappeared around a corner.

"I am ready for a comfy hotel bed," Ellis's mom said as she rejoined her parents.

"Agreed," Ellis said. As they headed off, Ellis cast one last look over her shoulder. She watched as the two women tried hard to explain themselves to the air marshal.

Ellis thought back to the long, bumpy flight. Without the turbulence, she realized, she wouldn't have seen Vanessa's hidden clothing. *Maybe thunderstorms at 30,000 feet aren't so bad after all,* she thought.

MY•PET

GLOSSARY

air marshal (AIR MAR-shuhl)—a law enforcement officer on an airplane who works undercover as a regular citizen to provide safety and security for other passengers

board (BOHRD)—to get into or on a vehicle such as an airplane, ship, or train

convention (kuhn-VEN-shuhn)—a large gathering of people who have the same interests

generation (jen-uh-RAY-shuhn)—all the members of a group of people born around the same time

insurance (in-SHU-ruhnss)—a contract between a person and a company to provide protection against loss or damage of one's property, health, or life

interview (IN-tur-vyoo)—to ask someone questions to find out more about something

red-eye (RED-eye)—an airline flight that departs late at night and arrives early in the morning

scheme (SKEEM)—a sneaky plan to do something unethical or illegal

tarmac (TAHR-mak)—a road, runway, or parking area at an airport

terminal (TER-muh-nuhl)—an area of an airport where passengers wait to board a plane

turbulence (TUR-byoo-luns)—strong, swirling winds that can cause rough bouncing and shaking on an airplane in flight

IT'S POSSIBLE

Flying Phantoms

"She's a ghost!" That's one explanation Ellis and Luke give for the missing passenger. But several people have claimed to see ghosts on real planes. Some even claimed to speak with the spooks!

In 1972 Eastern Air Lines Flight 401 crashed in the swampy Florida Everglades. One of the men who died that day was Captain Robert Loft. Undamaged parts from the plane were later used to replace parts on other planes. But on those planes, eerie things occurred.

On one flight a crew member claimed to see the face of Captain Loft in the microwave oven door. The phantom spoke: "Watch out for fire on this plane." On the return flight, one of the engines failed and was shut down before it could catch on fire. Were the passengers and crew saved by a phantom warning?

Spookier still was the ghost on a Virgin Atlantic plane. A flight attendant saw an old man standing in the plane's kitchen. He asked the attendant to give a message to a woman traveling on the plane. When the attendant gave the message, the woman pulled out a photo she carried. "That's him!" said the attendant. "That's my dead husband," said the woman. His body was in a coffin in the plane's cargo hold! The old man's message? "Tell her I'm okay."

DISCUSS IT

1. Bernice Waterson's sister, Vanessa, boarded the plane dressed in odd clothes, a dark wig, and pale makeup. What reason do you think she had for wearing such a strange disguise?

2. At the end of the story Luke returns the wallet he stole to its rightful owner. Why do you think he stole the man's wallet? Explain why you think he chose to give it back.

3. After the blue necklace disappears, Ellis thinks that Luke took it. Why would she think that he stole the necklace? What did Luke do or say to make Ellis think that he took it?

WRITE IT

1. Ellis loves mystery stories featuring the teen detective Kerri Keane. Write your own short story describing how Kerri Keane discovers some clues and solves a baffling mystery.

2. Have you ever flown on an airplane in bad weather? Did you think it was exciting or scary? Write a few paragraphs describing your trip and what it was like to fly through the storm.

3. Imagine you're traveling to a distant city. What would you do to keep your valuables safe? Write down a plan for how to protect your personal property while traveling to unfamiliar locations.

AUTHOR

Brandon Terrell is the author of numerous children's books. He has written several titles in the Michael Dahl Presents, Jake Maddox Graphic Novels, and Snoops, Inc. series. When not hunched over his laptop, Brandon enjoys watching movies and TV, reading, watching and playing baseball, and spending time with his wife and two children at his home in Minnesota.

ILLUSTRATOR

Amerigo Pinelli lives in the heart of Naples, Italy, among narrow streets and old churches. He studied in the Art School of Naples and the Comics School. After this he specialized in illustration at the International School of Illustration S. Zavřel. Amerigo has worked in both animation and publishing. He thinks making a living doing what he loves is a great gift, and he considers himself very lucky. His three daughters, Chiara, Teresa, and Irene, fill his life with color and joy. For Amerigo and his wife, Giulia, life is never boring.